BETRAY

BETH YARNALL

BETRAY

BETH YARNALL

BETRAY

Dedication

To my husband, Mr Y, for buying into and supporting every single one of my crazy Lucy and Ethel schemes...including the one where I thought I could write a book.

CONTENTS

1

I bolted awake, jack-knifing upright.

I searched the shadows, expecting the specter from my nightmare to be sitting at the foot of my bed.

I'd had this dream before.

Blinking hard, I tried to bring the room into focus. My heart beat frantically in my chest. My vision sharpened, but the outline of the man didn't fade.

"Good morning, Glory."

That voice.

Fear slammed into me a second time. Digging my heels into the mattress, I pushed myself as far back in the bed as I could.

"Where are you going?" He laughed, his voice unexpectedly rough and accusing. "I told you I'd be back." He made no move, yet his tone pinned me in place like a butterfly specimen.

I heard the strike a split second before the match lit his face, then extinguished. The room filled with the scent of fine tobacco. His scent. I swallowed the bile rising at the back of my throat.

"Did you think I wouldn't find you? I admit you gave me a chase. Changing your name, your looks. I liked that you made it difficult. A man appreciates a good hunt." He rose from the chair, but made no move toward me. Instead he walked to the dresser and picked up a framed photo.

"Who is he?" he asked with a calmness that made the hair at the nape of my neck prickle. I could feel his stare on me through the dimly lit room, an undeniable force. "Glory." His volume and tenor were unchanged yet I started at the sound of his pet name for me.

"A friend," I answered in measured tones.

"A friend." He dropped the photo, shattering the glass against the hardwood floor. "Am I not your friend, Glory?" His voice took on a new calmness that frightened me even more.

Pressed up hard against the headboard, I cautiously told him what I thought he wanted to hear. "Yes."

"Hmm." He seemed to consider my answer as he sucked hard on his cigarette, making it glow hot in the early morning darkness. He strolled to the other side of the room and picked up the black dress I'd discarded earlier in the evening. He rubbed it between his fingers then pressed it to his face, inhaling deeply. "The smell of you, that is unchanged." He turned toward me slowly. "I can smell you from here, Glory." The suggestiveness in his voice scattered goose bumps over my body.

I watched him with all the wariness of a fly trapped in a spider's web.

He threw the dress at me. "Put it on."

"What?"

"Really, Glory. You're caught. Do you not realize this?" He relaxed back into the chair he'd occupied earlier, propping his ankle on his knee. "Put. It. On." He took a hard drag then ground his cigarette out on the bottom of his shoe.

I debated going against him, but old memories had me quickly wriggling out of my nightgown and into the evening dress under the cover of the darkened room. Never taking my eyes off his shadowy shape, I adjusted the dress as best I could.

"Stand."

I did as I was told, scrambling off the far side of the bed.

"Turn the light on."

I panicked, taking a step back.

"Glory, my patience has an end," he warned.

Taking a breath, I clicked on the

bedside lamp, illuminating my face then my body as I stood to face him.

"Madre de Dios," he hissed, bolting out of his chair. He surged forward, forcing me against the window. The cold from the windowpane seeped through the curtains to my skin. He gripped my arm, shaking me. "What have you done?"

A new boldness brought my chin up and for the first time I let all the anger and helplessness he'd burdened me with for most of my adult life seep out as defiance. "What does it look like?"

He struck my face hard, knocking me to the floor. His kick sent me into the wall. I'd been dealt these blows before... and more.

"You stupid, bitch." He yanked me up by the front of my dress, his face inches from mine and in the lamplight I saw something I'd never seen before. Fear. Real fear. He shook me again, rattling my head like a ragdoll.

"Careful, Carlos. You wouldn't want to hurt the baby."

He released me, staring at the twist in

the front of my dress just above my gently rounded belly, horror turning his face pale. This close I could smell the stench of panicked sweat, mingling with his fine Mexican tobacco. I hadn't expected his reaction. If I had, I would have handled his return much differently.

He stepped back slowly, edging his way around the bed toward the door, watching me all the while. I stayed where I was, sensing my new vulnerability was the impetus for his escape.

I took my first real gulp of air as he disappeared through the doorway.

I broke into tears at the click of the front door closing behind him.

2

"Gia, I'm sorry. Baby, pick up the phone." I stared at the answering machine, waiting for his next words, which were always the same. "I had to work. David needed me to meet with the new investors. I tried to call, but you didn't answer. It was supposed to be a short meeting, but as usual David... Ah Jesus, Gia. I'm sorry."

Gia was close enough to Gina and far enough from Glory as I could possibly get and still remember it was my name now. I rubbed my belly, caressing the subtle roundness. Truett Nash was an insufferable ass who'd stood me up last night, but he was also the father of my baby. What could I do? I picked up the phone.

"Roses. Deep red. And dark chocolate."

"Gia. Baby, I'm so sorry."

"You always are."

"I know you're mad. I screwed up bad this time. I'm really sorry." He was sincere; I'd give him that. "I'll make it up to you. I promise." And he always did, which was how I'd come to be pregnant by him. "I'll take you for Thai food. Bring you those roses and chocolate. I missed you last night, baby."

I would have said I missed him too, but that would have been a lie. I was already lying to him about so many other things. My name. My background. Our relationship. I wondered when I would be free to tell the truth. To feel again. I stroked the soft curve of my belly, trying hard to imagine what an expectant mother was supposed to feel. I pressed my brain for memories of my own mother, but all I could come up with were vague impressions of a woman with brown eyes and soft skin.

"Gia?"

"Yes."

"I'll see you tonight. Seven o'clock. I won't be late. I promise."

"All right, Tru."

I hung up the phone before he could make more promises he might not keep. I couldn't be mad. He hadn't known it was my birthday. I'd never told him. I only told him what he needed to know, which was as little as possible.

I glanced around at the apartment I'd rented because it had come furnished and was close to Tru's office. I had nothing here that was truly mine. I'd worked hard to make the shabby furnishings look like a home, to make it appear as if someone really lived here. There were framed photos of people I'd printed off the Internet. An older couple, Gianfranco, my 'father' who'd I'd been named for and Maria, my 'mother', both supposedly dead now. A knitted afghan my 'grandmother' had made for me, but had actually been purchased at a garage sale, was draped over an arm of the couch. Other odds and ends were scattered about for show, a souvenir mug, an art class painting a 'friend' had given me, a lamp, an antique clock, and a hand-blown glass vase.

My thigh ached where Carlos had kicked me. I raised the hem of my night-gown to examine the deep purple mark. Truett would ask how I got it.

Scanning the room, my gaze came to rest on the small wooden desk in the corner. I measured the height of the desk corner against the bruise on my leg. It would be plausible enough. Plausibility was always a problem for me. I could be easily tripped up by plausibility.

My encounter last night with Carlos had proven that. He would be back, of that I was sure. I would have to be prepared.

I dressed quickly, not giving much thought to what I wore. What did it matter? This was how Gia dressed, not me. I pulled my darkened hair back into a tight ponytail that trailed down to the middle of my back. I preferred short, cropped hair, but Gia wore her hair long the way Tru liked it. Carlos thought I'd changed my look to hide from him, to extend the chase. How like him to think that.

Checking the time, I realized I only had twenty minutes. I grabbed my bag and hit the door, calculating the best route to take. I couldn't be late.

As I rounded the corner, I saw my contact fold his newspaper and walk away, leaving the bench empty except for the paper. I strolled up casually, keeping to my role as an early morning park visitor. Laying my bag on top of the newspaper, I unwrapped my bagel from its wax paper and bit into it. The park was relatively empty but for a lone male jogger, a mother of twins and myself. Out of the corner of my eye I watched the jogger pause at a fitness station then begin the exercise, his long legs easily making light work of the deep knee bends.

I pretended to watch the mother and

her toddlers enjoying the bright autumn day, while keeping track of the jogger until he jogged off down the path. He didn't reappear.

Finishing my bagel, I packed up my things, surreptitiously tucking the newspaper into my tote bag. Keeping an eye out for anyone who seemed out of place, I headed off to run errands.

My day had been like any other day except for the feeling that had grown stronger and stronger since I'd entered the park that morning—I was being watched. Even now, back in my apartment, the feeling persisted, pressing in on me.

I pulled a notebook and pen from my bag and began an arbitrary list. Twisting the top of the pen, I activated the wireless signal detector inside. This was not the first time I'd taken this step to protect myself. I'd been trained to perform this task whenever I returned to the apartment.

Wandering around casually, tapping

the pen against my chin as if thinking, the detector did not locate a signal in the living area. I moved to the bedroom and bath, repeating the process. I didn't get so much as a blip, but the feeling of eyes on me never eased, staying with me the rest of the day.

Truett arrived in a rush, as he always did, twenty minutes late, spouting apologies. "I'm really sorry. I know you..." He cut off, taking in my appearance from head to toe then back again.

I stood in the doorway, barring his entrance, wearing a low cut, soft cotton dress in an amber shade that brought out the golden tones of my deeply tanned skin. I'd taken the time to curl my hair, letting it tumble around my shoulders and down my back. Tru's face would go from stunned to immensely pleased whenever he saw me as if I were a present he'd just opened. I liked that look. I liked a lot of things about him.

"Here." He thrust a small bouquet of deep red, nearly black roses at me. "And here." He produced a bar of dark chocolate from his pocket, offering it with a shy, abashed smile.

I accepted his gifts, taking a moment to touch the soft petals and enjoy their scent.

"Am I forgiven?" he asked with all the glint-eyed repentance of a schoolboy caught tugging the pigtails of the girl in front of him.

In answer to his question, I stepped back, allowing his admittance.

He closed the door, then turned me, backing me up against it. "Gia." He whispered softly, his hands sliding up my arms to cup my face. "I missed you."

Then his lips were on mine. The kiss began slowly, as his kisses always do, building and building until we both were a little out of breath. He pulled back gradually, his focus connecting with mine in a frisson of awareness that had me melting into the door and him sagging further against me.

If I had to choose only one man to kiss for the rest of my life that man would be Truett Nash. But my life was not filled with choices.

He placed his hand gently on my abdomen and asked, "How are you?"

This intimacy was difficult for me. I'd given my body to him in just about every way, but these emotions, the ones that dug deep, I held back.

Pasting on a teasing smile, I wriggled out of his grasp and reached for my bag. "Hungry," I answered.

If he noticed my avoidance, he didn't let it show. Instead, he flashed me a bashful grin the one that had attracted me to him from the start, and while his smile still drew me, it now came with an accompanying pang of guilt.

"I'm sorry. You must be starving." He helped me into my sweater, leaning in to place a kiss on the curve of my neck. "Still want Thai food?"

I'd been craving the contrasting flavors of spicy Pad Thai and the creamy sweetness of Thai iced tea almost since the moment I'd conceived. "Mmm. I can't wait. Give me a moment to put these in water."

I pulled the vase I'd bought that afternoon at a thrift store in anticipation of his flowers, out of the cabinet. I filled it with water and arranged the roses. I ran my fingertips across the velvety bouquet, treasuring it. I'd received few gifts in my life, certainly none I could keep.

"If I'd known how you'd react, I'd have bought a larger bunch."

I looked up to find Tru watching me, a puzzled line between his brows. I schooled my expression, fearing I'd divulged something to him I shouldn't have. "I don't think I've ever seen such a deep red before. They're really beautiful."

"I'm glad you like them." His face broke into an easy, open smile, the kind I'd never been allowed. His expressions often revealed what he was thinking or feeling. It was like peering into the looking glass of his soul, he hid nothing, sharing everything. I liked that about him, too.

"Thank you." I moved into his arms

easily, smoothing a lock of dark auburn hair from his forehead and kissed him lightly. "Shall we go?"

He reached for my hand and brought it to his lips before tugging me out the door.

House of Palm was a tiny family style Thai restaurant just three blocks from my apartment and next door to the coffee house where I'd 'met' Tru. Multi colored paper lanterns swayed gently under the breeze created by palm frond-bladed ceiling fans. Large palm leaves created a canopy over our booth upholstered in sparkly gold-flecked vinyl tufted with large gold buttons.

I already knew what I wanted to eat so I took a moment to observe Tru.

He had a boyishness about him that fascinated me. His hair was always a little too long and often hung in his eyes, tangling with his eyelashes. He swiped at it frequently, an unconscious gesture that I found endearing. I wondered briefly if our baby would look like him. I hoped so. I'd played so many roles for so long I wasn't entirely sure what I looked like anymore.

He caught me staring and grinned, his green eyes creasing a little at the corners. He was a good-looking man. I remembered being relieved about that when I'd received his dossier.

I returned his smile, letting some of what I'd been thinking about him leak out into it.

He laid down his menu and reached for my hand. "I like it when you look at me like that. It gives me all kinds of ideas."

"You're always having all kinds of ideas," I said, laying a hand over my belly. "Which is why I make you eat Thai food almost every night now."

His smiled dimmed a bit. "We haven't talked a lot about the future. About the baby, I mean. Do you... that is, um, will you move in with me?"

I immediately shook my head and his lips evened out, his expression closing. I had a brief moment of panic. *Keep him interested. Stay with him. Find out every-*

thing he knows, what he's working on. And don't fuck it up.

Right. Okay.

I kept my gaze on his, knowing what I had to do. "I'm sorry. I shouldn't have said no right away." His eyes remained steady on mine, but I could see that I'd hurt him. "I've never lived with anyone before. I'm not sure I'd be good at it, but if you're willing to take me on then... okay." The lies came so easily to me, he bought them right away, his happiness returning tenfold.

"When? My place or yours?" He bounced a little in his seat, his excitement growing. "I was thinking my place because it's bigger. But if you want to stay in your apartment, we could make it work. I was just thinking, with the baby coming we could turn my guest room into a nursery..." He jabbered on, but I couldn't match his enthusiasm. He wasn't going to get all of the things he wanted with me.

I put up a good front for him, nodding and agreeing to every suggestion he made. All the while I knew I was drawing him in, closer and closer. An uneasy feeling settled over me.

I was going to hurt him. And knowing that hurt me.

Looking at him across the table, planning for our future, for our baby, I longed for everything he offered me. I watched him and ached with the knowledge that I'd done the one thing I never should have done.

I'd fallen in love with Truett Nash.

A WEEK later I moved in with Tru.

Carlos hadn't visited again. I'd done what I could to stop him, but I knew it would only be temporary. Carlos was not one to let go. It had taken him the better part of a year to find me this time. I'd covered my tracks well, using my own contact to acquire a new identity, new paperwork. But he dogged me, lurking in the shadows as I walked down the street. The feeling of being watched never left me, not even while I slept.

Gasping for breath, I sat up abruptly in bed.

Tru was by my side in a flash, comforting me. "Gia, baby. It's all right. I'm here. You're fine."

I put a hand on his chest, pushing him back to protect him, searching for Carlos in the shadows of our bedroom.

"Gia."

I turned to him in the darkness, needing the comfort he offered. My body slickened with the sweat of fear I came up hard against him, knocking him back in the bed.

He accepted me willingly, gladly. I liked that about him. I liked that he could make me forget. Under his hands, his mouth, his thrusting body, I forgot Glory and the things she'd done. I forgot Gina and the things she'd never have. And I became Gia, who had everything and nothing. Nothing but Truett Nash and this night.

He found my mouth through the pitch black, through my deceit. I gripped him hard and he tumbled me over, taking me some place where I was everything he wanted and needed. I was his Gia, free and willing. I could give him this if nothing else. This was real and raw. This was everything and nothing. This was all I had.

He touched me in the dark, taking his time as if we had an infinite supply. I used my hands, my mouth to memorize him. The hard planes of his chest and back, the tight sinewy strength of his arms, the fleshy feel of his back side as he nudged at my opening and the coarseness of the hair on his legs, pushing mine further apart. I tried to burn it all into my memory.

He whispered to me in the dark, of my beauty, and of how much he wanted me. I'd never before felt so cherished. And when I spread my legs wide for him, offering him this if nothing else, he gave me more. More than I could ever give him. Each thrust, each kiss and tender murmur tore at me until I was screaming in pain or pleasure I wasn't sure. All I was sure of was Truett Nash. Inside and out, he surrounded me. In that moment where we came together I wanted to confess it all, tell him what I'd done and who I was. But I knew in doing so I'd lose him forever.

He slumped against me, breathing hard and heavy. And I couldn't stand it. I pushed at him, panicked in a way I hadn't felt before. I kicked and shoved until he rolled off me in shocked silence.

I ran for the bathroom and locked the door behind me. Collapsing down to the floor, I broke into hot shameful tears.

"Gia? Gia, open the door." He tried the knob then banged on the door. "Are you all right? I'm sorry. I thought... Gia. Open the door." I could almost feel the panic in his voice. "Gia, did I hurt you? Please, baby, open the door. Let me see." He hit the door hard, knocking my head against it on the other side. "Gia." He strung out my name like a plea.

I grabbed a towel and pressed my face into, smothering my sobs. What was I doing? To him, to myself? I hadn't gained the information I was supposed to have. I needed more time, I'd told them. He's just beginning to trust me, I insisted. They looked at me and my gently rounded belly and they'd given me three weeks.

If you don't have what we need by then, you're out.

Then the one who'd raised me and trained me, looked at me like I had wasted all his effort. "What will you do about your condition? You're of no use to us the way you are."

"I..." Glancing down at the soft swell of my belly I had a moment of clarity. "You could leave me in longer. Like you said, I'm of no use to you on another case. I need more time. My condition can give me that. We're moving in together. I'll have more access to him, to his work." I stood calmly and waited while they debated my future, but inside I was a jumbled mess.

"Gia, please." Tru's voice broke through to me.

I eased away from the door and unlocked it. Tru was through it in a flash, rushing to comfort me. "Are you hurt? Did I hurt you or the baby?"

I swiped at my tears. "I'm fine. Hormones I guess. I'm not hurt."

His hands swept over me, my face and hair, shoulders and back. "Jesus." He leaned back against the doorframe and flipped on the light.

I blinked hard against the glare, holding my hands in front of my eyes.

He trailed a finger along the slope of my neck. "I bit you." He sounded as surprised as I felt.

I tried to see the mark, but couldn't. He helped me to rise and face the mirror. We were a battered pair. I'd scratched his chest, four perfect lines. His razor burn marred my breasts and neck along with the bite. I studied him, standing just over my left shoulder, his face flushed with concern and the lingering intensity of our passion. And I almost did it. I almost told him everything.

He brushed the hair back from my face with his hands, smoothing it down my back. Then he reached around, holding me against him, his palm flat against the swell of my stomach.

"Are you sure you're okay?" He pressed a kiss to the side of my neck, just below my ear.

"I'm fine. I promise." I placed my hand over his on my belly. "Hormones I'm sure." I silently berated myself for my stupidity. Telling him would only endanger us both.

"Come back to bed." He led me back to his bed, tucking me tight against him. "Gianfranco."

"What?"

"For the baby, if it's a boy we could name him after your father."

"No." My 'father' was a man who didn't exist.

Tru shifted so we were side by side. "Tell me what you want."

"What do you mean?"

He smoothed the hair away from my face. "What do you want... with me? Because Gia, I want to marry you and I need to know if that's what you want to."

My chest tightened, denial fixed in

the back of my throat. I swallowed hard, forcing it down. "Are you asking me to marry you?"

He reached for my hand, bringing it to his chest. "I am."

I looked down to where our hands were clasped over his heart. Emotions crowed my chest, elbowing each other for equal space– hope, dread, desire, fore-boding, love, fear and a yearning so strong it made my breath hitch.

"I can do the bended knee thing." He squeezed my hand and rolled away. I heard the bedside drawer open, then he was back, pressing a small box into my hand. Kneeling on the bed beside me, he held my hand in both of his. "Gia, will you marry me?"

I couldn't find my voice.

I should tell him no. That would've been the kind thing to do. But I'd never been taught kindness. Only how to survive and how to do the job. In the meager light from the streetlight coming through the crack in the curtains I could just make out the hope in his expression. Not just hope...

"I love you," he said, bringing my hands to his lips for a kiss. "Please be my wife. Make us a family."

I knew we were being monitored. I'd set up the surveillance devices myself. They were listening, recording my progress and my lack of progress. Knowing that and how any promise I made today would be void tomorrow I did something stupid and reckless.

"Yes," I whispered, foolishly trying to keep my response for his ears only.

He slid a ring on my finger and kissed my hand again. Then his lips found mine and we tumbled back down on the bed.

"Do you love me?" There was desperation in his voice.

My answer wouldn't change anything. He'd marry me whether I loved him or not. For responsibility. For the baby. For the love he had for me. Truett Nash was not one to shirk his obligations. His drive, his one mindedness, and relentlessness were what had catapulted him to the top of his field. It was also the reason I was in his bed.

When it was over he'd look back and try to pinpoint the moments when he should've seen who and what I was. I wouldn't let this be one of those moments.

"Yes. Very much."

"Oh, baby. You don't know…"

"I do know."

When *I* would look back at our time together I'd always remember this moment as the truest, most honest exchange we'd ever have. For now I was Gia and Tru was my fiancé. As we made plans for the future I threw myself into them as though they'd really come true. We made love a second time slow and easy like two people who had the forever they dreamed about. I fell head first into the illusion and for the first time in my life I hoped.

ON THE WALLS in Truett's home office were large framed displays of butterflies.

His favorite was the one that hung behind his desk. It was a collection of North African butterflies. He'd been stationed there *somewhere*. That's all he'd ever told me and only because I'd asked about the butterflies. Of course I already knew about his time there and what he'd done, what he continued to do. It was the reason I was here.

I stood behind him while he sat at the desk and spoke on the phone with his mother, making wedding plans. I couldn't bring myself to be a part of their conversation so I focused on the butterflies. Fine pins held them in place where they'd stay mounted there forever, never to flutter their wings or breathe free air. I was like the butterflies, pinned down and forced to be where I was. The colors in their wings fascinated me. Something so vibrant and ethereal shouldn't be held under glass for so few to enjoy.

The baby moved within me. Instinctively I placed a protective hand over swollen abdomen. Behind me Tru laughed at something his mother must have said. The sound made me turn away from the butterflies to watch the way his face changed when he smiled. He rarely laughed. Neither did I. We were such serious people, doing serious things. The fine lines around his eyes deepened. He looked up at me and placed his hand over mine on his shoulder. His smile was contagious and I found myself unable to keep the corners of my mouth from tipping up.

I could hear his mother's, then his father's voice across the line. We stayed that way, staring at each other, goofy grins creasing our faces until he disconnected the call.

"They want us to have the wedding in their backyard. Dad says he'll build a gazebo." He slid back from the desk and pulled me down into his lap. "They can't wait to meet you."

"Why?"

His smile faded away and his brows drew together. "Because you're about to be my wife and the mother of my child, their grandchild."

When he examined my face, as he was now, a knot of fear twisted in my belly. Had he caught me in a lie? Did I somehow slip up? Was he on to me?

"Don't look so terrified, Gia. They'll love you." He smoothed a hand over my stomach. "And our baby."

"I know. I guess...I guess I'm just nervous about meeting them." Two more people to trick and lie to.

"Don't be. They'll love you as much as I do." He looked down to where his hand rested over our child. "Or is there something else you're worried about?"

"No." I moved out of his embrace and toward the door. "I just want them to like me."

"They will."

With one last glance at the butterflies forever frozen in death I made up an excuse about needing something from the store and promised to be back soon. I hadn't thought about this part of things when I'd agreed to marry him. I hadn't thought about any of it. This wasn't like me. It was my duty to consider every aspect of the job, leave nothing to chance. Chastising myself for my stupidity—or was it wishful thinking?—I almost missed it. He disappeared around the corner, leaving nothing but a fleeting glimpse. Ordinary people wouldn't have noticed him, but he lived in my nightmares, making me hyper aware of his presence. For a split second I froze like those butter-flies under glass. He'd always been the pin that had held me in place no matter how hard I struggled.

No more.

I crossed the street, dodging cars, causing them to honk their horns and gesture rudely. New Yorkers weren't the type to go with the flow. But I didn't care. He wasn't going to get away this time. I was pulling out the pin that held me in place. Breaking into a run, I rounded the corner in time to see him enter the back entrance of the building across from Tru's.

Carlos had found me.

Again.

I skidded to a stop outside the door

he'd disappeared through. The baby did a tumble in my belly, reminding me of what was at stake. Adrenaline coursed through me. I'd learned long ago how to override its effects and ignore the fight or flight instinct. Making quick work of the lock, I went down the hall, keeping my senses sharp. One floor up a door closed. I scanned the narrow corridor for cameras or other security measures. I wasn't surprised to not find any. He wouldn't expect me to go after him. That wasn't the game. It was always him chasing after me, controlling me. Every time I escaped he always came for me.

His reliance on my fear of him, of the repercussions, was going to work against him. I'd been a fool for him once, letting him control every aspect of my life. When I'd become pregnant by him he'd made me abort it. He didn't want any brats interfering with his work or my time with him. He especially didn't want any marks on my body or be denied access to it whenever he wanted. He was selfish like that. My current pregnancy was a defiance I hadn't known I was capable of. I wanted this baby. He wasn't going to take it from me.

We worked for the same people. He knew what the job required. When we'd been together he slept with women outside the job just because he could. Me using my body to complete a mission like I was doing with Tru was something he'd learned to accept, but as soon as the job was over I was under his thumb again. Getting pregnant by Tru broke that cycle. Even though my pregnancy was the ultimate betrayal Carlos still thought of me as his.

Not anymore.

I reached the top of the landing and paused. There were four apartments on this floor. *He* was behind one of those doors. I walked past the first door without stopping to listen. My intuition pulled me toward the third door. The windows would look out onto the street and give a clear view of the front of Tru's apartment. It wasn't this logical deduction that drew me to the yellow door with the chipped paint. I could *feel* him behind it. The air around the door seemed to pulse with the energy of the man who'd been my lover, my mentor, my tormentor.

There was a flurry of movement in my belly as if the baby was trying to warn me. I crept closer anyway, undeterred and more determined than ever. This was going to end here and now.

3

Carlos didn't seem surprised to see me. He turned slowly toward the door, the backlight from the window casting his face in shadows. The twenty or so feet between us were filled with a lifetime of wrongs and rights, love and hate, resentment and necessity. When I looked at him I saw myself at eighteen, young and fragile and so full of myself I thought nothing bad could ever happen to me. A whole lot of not good had happened to me and the majority of it lay at Carlos's door. I chose him. I chose to go with him. I chose to link my path to his. And every one of those choices had led me to Truett Nash and to this moment.

"If you think I'll take you back like that—" He gestured toward my pregnancy.

"No. I know you won't. I don't want you to."

"Is that why you did it?"

"Believe it or not it was an accident."

"You're not supposed to have 'accidents'. I know the one you had with me wasn't."

"No, it wasn't." I stepped into the room and let the door close behind me. I expected fear, but I was strangely hollow inside.

"You wanted to tie me down."

"I wanted a life. I still do."

"Is that why you didn't get rid of this one?"

"He didn't want me to. He wants this baby."

"Of course he does. He wants you even though he doesn't know you." He moved away from the window, pulled a cigarette out of a pack on the table, and lit it.

Smoke curled around him, making him look mysterious and powerful. My body reacted to the scent of his tobacco like Pavlov's dog. A trickle of moisture dampened my underpants and my nipples pressed against the cups of my bra. My stupid, traitorous body. I thought of Tru and the look on his face as he slid into me. An even more powerful wave of desire swept over me.

"Come here." He didn't crook his finger, but he may as well have.

I didn't even try to stop myself from moving toward him. I *wanted* to be closer to him. I wanted to look into his eyes. I wanted to smell like I'd been smoking his cigarettes.

"Why?" he asked.

"I don't want the things I used to."

"Like me?"

"And the life. I can't lie the way I used to."

"You're nothing but a lie to him. None of it is real. Only I know the real you."

"And yet my pregnancy surprised you."

He narrowed his eyes and blew out a stream of smoke over his shoulder. "You're a fool. They're never going to let you go and do you honestly think *he's* going to want you when he finds out who you are and what you've done?"

"Maybe not."

"They'll kill you. That's the only way out."

"Not the only way."

His eyes widened with surprise. "You traitorous bitch. You're not the only one with your dick out here."

"You think I care what happens to you?"

"You think I'm going to let you betray me, leave me hanging?"

"No." I eased closer. "I know you won't."

"You have a death wish then."

He bent to stub out his cigarette as I brought my arm forward, swinging with everything I had. The knife plunged deep. His gaze flew up to mine, his face stark with shock. Before he could move I yanked the knife back and swung again. His hand went to the wound as he teetered back. I didn't give him time to recover. Pulling out another knife, I got him in the back, bringing him down onto the coffee table. The legs broke and he crashed to the ground without a sound.

Knives in both hands, I couldn't stop. Over and over I struck him. Blood flung out in all directions. Long stripes of it covered the walls, the furniture. Raw, animalistic sounds ripped from my throat with the force of my blows. His blue shirt turned deep red and still I didn't stop. I couldn't stop. Every indignity, every time I'd cowered before him, every time he'd made me do something I didn't want to do poured out of me and into my attack.

I finally collapsed in exhaustion, my knives protruding from his body. His eyes were open, staring and fixed. I wondered what he had thought as I struck him. He'd been too surprised to stop me. I had never gone against him. Not ever until my pregnancy. Maternity had changed me.

Seeing his reaction the night he snuck into my room started something that ended here in this generic apartment. I was free. I couldn't help the laugh that escaped me. It filled the room and bounced off the blood-streaked walls. If Tru saw me now he'd think I'd gone insane. Maybe I had. Carlos's death wouldn't be the end of it.

It was only the beginning.

4

Before leaving Carlos's apartment, I cleaned myself up as best as I could. I wiped away any evidence that I'd been there, including pulling my knives from Carlos's body. He'd taught me well. I didn't go straight home. Instead I wandered aimlessly, watching to make sure no one was following me. It was dark by the time I entered Tru's apartment. A relieved breath whooshed out of me as I closed the door and leaned back against it. Carlos was dead.

I would never be the same again.

Killing him made me feel strangely

adrift. Tru's ring on my finger was the only thing anchoring me to the here and now, reminding me of the tasks that still lay ahead. My job with Tru was unfinished. I couldn't just walk away from it. That's not how things worked. Carlos's death bought me some time. A plan had been formulating in my mind for some time. At first I'd chided myself for being so foolish as to hope for a life with Tru. Now it not only felt possible it felt close enough to touch. I could marry Tru and have his baby. I could have the happily ever after I'd only read about in romance novels.

I showered and bleached the drain. The clothes I wore went into the fireplace. They smoked and crackled. It was like watching Carlos die all over again. I brought my blouse up to my nose and inhaled. The scent of his tobacco lingered along with the metallic stench of his blood mixed in with the perfume I wore. It seemed symbolic that this was the last time he and I would ever be joined. I tossed the blouse onto the fire and prodded at it with the fireplace poker. It couldn't burn fast enough.

Just as I replaced the poker and the last of the pale pink browned then disappeared, Truett came through the door. As usual there was a harried, disconnected air about him. His mind was still on his work. I watched him juggle binders and a briefcase and his laptop case across the living room until he dumped the whole mess onto the bar between the kitchen and dining area. He ran a distracted hand through his hair. There was a deep crease between his eyes and his lips pressed together. Something was wrong.

He didn't notice me until I stood, wrapped in my bathrobe, my feet bare, and my hair damp from the shower. His mouth relaxed, but his brows still crowded together.

"Oh, hey. I didn't see you there," he said, his attention focused inward.

"Everything okay?"

"Yeah." He shook his head. "Not really. No."

I strode over to him. He wasn't so

distracted that he didn't notice that I wasn't wearing anything beneath the robe.

I wrapped my arms around his neck. "Anything I can help you with?"

"Work stuff."

I willed my body not to tense under his hands at my waist. "Is it very bad?"

"A file's missing. Not really missing just...not right. Somebody messed with it."

"Messed with it how?" But I knew how. I'd been given the thumb drive with a duplicated file embedded with a Trojan horse. It had done its work when Tru connected his computer to the main server.

"A worm or a Trojan horse they think. They're working on it now. I came home to see if I could find out how it got onto my laptop. It's the only way I can think that it happened. I need to find out before I tell them it was me."

"Are you sure it's from your computer?"

"Yeah. I'm sure."

Dread licked my insides, turning my stomach queasy. "How?"

His gaze met mine and the dread turned to fear. Did he know it was me? Did he know that what I'd unleashed could ruin him *and* us? That in order to get out I'd gotten up from our bed last night as soon as he'd drifted off to do one last thing, one last betrayal on a long list of lies and hidden agendas?

"Because I have systems in place to let me know when someone's messed with my computer." He took a step forward, forcing me to take a step back. "Some-one's after what they think is on it." He moved us backward a couple of paces. "It took me a while to figure that out." Another step and my back hit the wall. He pressed the full weight of his body against mine and braced his forearm on the wall above my head. His other hand twisted in the belt of my robe. He ducked his head and ran his tongue from the hollow of my neck to just behind my ear. I shuddered and fisted my hands in his shirt. "But I figured it out."

He knew. Not only that he knew his apartment was bugged.

I lowered my voice so only he could hear. "What did you figure out?"

"Not enough. Not soon enough."

"What is it that you think you've figured out?"

"Who are you?" His whispered words against my ear made me shiver all over again. "Who are you really?"

I brought his head down and put my lips to his ear. "Not here."

This was it. Time to confess.

"Where?" His lack of anger and accusation was confusing. As was his arousal pressed against my hip.

My head thunked against the wall as I pulled as far away from him as I could and raised my voice to a normal level. "I need to pick up a few things from the store for dinner. Want to walk with me and clear your head?"

"Yeah. Let's do that."

5

"How about a walk in the park?" Tru asked as we left his apartment.

I glanced up at the second floor window of the building across the street, but it wasn't relief I felt. When they found out Carlos was dead I would be too.

"That sounds nice," I agreed.

It was a risk. There were verdant areas of Central Park where a body wouldn't be discovered for days, weeks even, if ever. I hadn't considered myself maternal. Mostly I found pregnancy to be confusing and sometimes frustrating. As we entered the park I realized that if it came down to him or me I would kill the father of my child. I could only hope his paternal instinct would suddenly kick in as mine had.

"What gave me away?"

The question hovered in the air around us. We stared straight ahead down the nearly deserted path. Nothing between us had ever been honest. There had been so many lies I wasn't sure if I'd recognize the truth once I met it. But here was the moment to come clean. There was no other way around it.

"There was a slight flaw in your background."

He looked at me then. "Were you the one who caught it?"

"Yes."

"What was it?"

"Truett Nash wasn't left handed."

"Shit." He shook his head. "I'm usually better than that."

"I know."

"So are you. Why so careless with my laptop? That's not like you."

"I wanted to get caught."

He stopped and pulled me down onto a bench. The sun was low in the sky casting long, pale shadows. The summer air still held the heat of midday and the stifling closeness of humidity.

"Why?" he asked, his gaze searched my face no doubt looking for any trace of dishonesty.

"They were going to pull me off you. They didn't like that I got pregnant. It complicated things."

He placed his hand on the swell of my stomach. "No kidding. I don't usually make these kinds of mistakes."

"Neither do I." I placed my hand over his. "Now what?"

"I was hoping you would have an answer."

"I'm supposed to kill you."

"*I'm* supposed to kill *you*."

"You may as well. I'm dead anyway. They know I outed myself. They've probably already dispatched someone to take care of me."

Plus the fact that I'd killed one of their best agents when I'd stabbed Carlos to death. There was no going back from that. My only hope was to reveal myself to Tru. Either he'd kill me or I didn't know what. I'd rather he kill me than the agency. A strange statement to make, I know, but I'd accept death from Tru. At least then I'd know if what we'd shared meant as much to him as it did to me. I didn't want to die not knowing that.

"You're good. If you hadn't given yourself away I might have never known you were after me. I can't kill someone as good as you. That would be sacrilege. Plus there's this." His gaze fell to where our hands covered the swell of the child we'd made together.

"Yeah." My voice was breathy with pent up emotion. "There is."

"You want this baby?"

I nodded. "You?"

"More than I thought possible."

"Where does that leave us? They'll come after you as soon as they've taken care of me. The people I work for don't like loose ends."

"Neither do the people I work with.

We're doubly marked." He placed the palm of his other hand on my cheek. "I love you, Gia, or whatever your name is."

"I love you, Truett, or whatever your name is."

"I have a contingency plan, a way out."

"So do I. Are we really doing this? Or are you biding time for a better time and place to kill me?"

"We are unless you're biding time for a better time and place to kill me."

"I bet my contingency plan is better than yours."

"I bet it is." He placed a gentle kiss on my lips. "Are you still going to marry me?"

I kissed him back, needing the reassuring pressure of his mouth on mine to know that what was between us was real, that this was really going to happen. "Yes, I am."

He stood and held his hand out to me. "Paris is nice this time of year. None of this New York humidity."

I stood and took his hand. "I'm partial to Brunei."

"Brunei it is then."

The sun dipped below the trees as we made our plans. It wouldn't be easy, it was certainly risky, but Truett Nash and I were going to carve out our own version of happily ever after. Just the three of us.

*****

Thank you for reading BETRAY! If you love my DANGEROUS LINES series, you'll love the sexy, funny, award nomi-nated INNOCENT serial. Cora's brother was convicted of a murder he didn't commit and it's up to Cora to set him free. Inspired by real cases.

★Nominated in 2017 for the Romance Writers of America Rita® award★

➤One-click EPISODE ONE Now➤

THERE ARE seven books in the DANGEROUS LINES series.

➤One-click to see if you missed any! ➤

If you enjoyed Betray, please consider

leaving a review on your favorite book site. Reviews help readers find books!

➤BETRAY (DANGEROUS LINES series)➤

➤GOODREADS➤

Join my VIP Facebook group Babes with Books for exclusive sneak peeks at my upcoming books & other, members only, perks:

➤www.facebook.com/groups/Babes-WithBooksReaderGroup

Sign up to receive my newsletter for new release alerts, exclusive bonus content, and giveaways!

➤**www.bethyarnall.com/newsletter**

Turn the page to read an excerpt from INNOCENT: EPISODE ONE now!

EXCERPT FROM INNOCENT: EPISODE ONE

Cora

I got my driver's license on my sixteenth birthday so I could visit my brother in prison. California Institute for Men in Chino, California, sounds like one of those super-snooty colleges you have to be rich to get into or else be the next generation in a long line of alumni. But this is no college. Chino Men's, as it's referred to, is one of the most violent prisons in the state.

That's where they sent my brother to serve out his life sentence.

Five and a half years later, I've made the nearly two-hour trip from San Diego to Chino and back close to a hundred times. Four hours of driving to spend an hour—or more, if I'm lucky—with my brother. If I've gotten too late a start and visiting hours are over before my number is called or if Beau's visitation has been revoked because he's done something stupid, I don't get to see him at all.

I don't count those times.

"Seventy-three," one of the corrections officers intones.

I stand and give my number to the guard, like I'm in a deli about to order lunch or something.

"Name," he says.

"Cora Hollis."

"Inmate."

"Beau Hollis."

"Relationship."

"Sister." You'd think he'd recognize me by now. I've been here so many times. But every time he acts like it's my first visit and puts me through the same drill.

I've already been through the metal detector, searched, and patted down so thoroughly I'm questioning my sexuality.

Another guard comes over to lead me to a room full of lockers where I stow my cell-phone and car keys. Then I finally get to follow him to the visiting room, where Beau is already waiting for me.

Sometimes it takes me a moment to recognize him. He looks so unlike my brother. This bullshit prison has stolen more than years from Beau's life. It's robbed him of his dignity and anything resembling happiness.

I want to give him a hug, but that's not allowed. Instead, I drop into my seat opposite him. "I put twenty extra dollars in your commissary account this month."

Beau looks away, picking at the side of his thumb with his index finger. Even as a kid he always did this whenever he was agitated or annoyed. "I don't need it."

"I thought—"

His narrowed gaze swings back to me. It's his mean big-brother look, the one he always tries to intimidate me with. It didn't work when we were kids and it doesn't work now.

"I don't need a present," he says. "You need the money more."

"Yeah, well, I can't take it back out, so you're stuck with it. Happy birthday."

"Some fucking birthday."

"I'd have brought some pointy hats and balloons, but they wouldn't fit up my ass."

"Watch your fucking mouth." He's barely two years older than me, but he's always taken the job of big brother seriously. Even after all he's been through.

"You're a fantastic example," I tell him.

I mean it as a joke, but it falls flat as Beau's ever-roaming gaze takes in the room around us. Since being incarcerated, my once fun-loving prankster of a brother has turned into a suspicious, twitchy, hypervigilant, hardened prisoner. I don't dare comment on the fading bruise under his left eye or his freshly sheared hair. He always looked like he needed a haircut even after an appointment with the barber. But that was before.

Before he was arrested, then convicted for the brutal rape, sodomy, and murder of his ex-girlfriend Cassandra. Before our family was torn apart and life as we knew it changed forever. Before I watched, helpless, as my brother turned into someone I hardly recognize anymore.

"Yeah, I'm not exactly winning Best Big Brother of the Year this year or any year, am I?"

I hate it when he puts himself down. "You're at the top, as far as I'm concerned."

He makes a rude noise, but doesn't comment.

"Did you get my card?" I ask.

"I got it. Thanks. How's school going?"

"I'm taking a really great online class this summer." I never got around to telling him that I quit school last year to work and save money for a possible appeal of his case. Or that the job I took is in a law office, where I have ample access to the law library and case reviews.

"It's not on something stupid like

criminal law or how to be a private investigator, is it?"

I shift in my seat.

"Aww, shit, Cora. You promised you'd give up on the stupid idea that you could get me out of here. Why are you wasting your time? I'm a lost cause. Everyone knows it. Take those beauty classes like you always wanted. Face the fact that you can't do what Mom's and Dad's lawyers and the public defender couldn't. I'm done. You're not. You still have a life."

"I don't believe that, Beau, and neither should you. Those charges were bullshit then and they're bullshit now. You didn't kill her. There's no way I'll ever believe it and I'm never going to stop looking for a way to get you out of here."

"Doesn't really matter if I did it or not. I'm convicted, aren't I?"

"I wasn't going to tell you this because I knew what you'd say, but I think I might have a new lead."

He holds up a hand. "Stop it. Stop it, right now."

I ignore him and continue. "I think I found a witness who could—"

"Damn it, Cora! I told you to stop."

His outburst has a couple of the guards coming off the wall where they've been leaning and looking at him hard. Beau waves them back and takes a deep breath, scrubbing his hands over his face.

"My life is ruined," he finally says. I hate it when he talks like this. I refuse to believe that he'll never get out of here. I refuse to believe that the criminal justice system that failed him won't ever redeem itself by righting its wrong and setting him free.

"Your life isn't," he continues. "I don't want any more of this to touch you. For fuck's sake, let it go." He leans across the table at me. His look and tone turn threatening. "Let it go." Then he gets up from the table and heads for the door that will take him back to his cell, ending our visit.

"Happy birthday!" I call after him. "I love you!"

He doesn't respond or acknowledge

me in any way. His mind is already back on the cell block. I've screwed up this visit and his birthday. I have to find a way to make it up to him, but I know nothing short of getting him out of this hellhole will make it right.

As I stand to leave, I wonder why I bother with these visits. He never seems to enjoy them, is never glad to see me. If anything, he appears to be annoyed and inconvenienced by my visits. He's given up on himself just as our mother, then our father, gave up on him. Maybe, I think, as I burst out of the prison and into the blazing mid-afternoon sun, I keep up the visits to give us both something we haven't had in a long, long time—hope.

But hope is a dangerous thing to court when there's nothing to support it. Sometimes it almost feels as if I'm tipping headfirst into a kind of vicious insanity where I keep doing the same things over and over, expecting different results. It's no way to live, but it's my life. And it's Beau's until I can figure out a way to get him out of here.

I climb into my car and curse its lack of air-conditioning. I have the money to fix it, but it's not my money—it's Beau's. So I roll down the windows and crank up the radio over the sound of the wind and head for home.

Some NPR talking head begins the hour with one of those feel-good stories that people like to repost over and over on social media. About how there really is good in the world and good in people. But with the prison behind me, and a long, hot drive ahead of me, I'm finding it hard to believe there's anything good or just here or anywhere else in the world.

Something the host says has me cranking up the sound on my crappy radio as high as it will go.

"—your work with The Freedom Project led to the release of Maurice Battle after he spent nearly forty years in prison for a crime he didn't commit."

I jerk the wheel and skid to a stop on the shoulder. A cloud of dust comes up around the car and into my rolled-down windows. I cough, scrambling for the

notebook I always keep in my bag, as the
man being interviewed answers.

"Our agency takes on one pro bono
case per year. We devoted as much time,
energy, and effort toward this case as we
do all of our cases. We're thrilled that our
work led to the exoneration of Mr.
Battle."

"What agency?" I scream at the radio,
my pen poised to write it down.

They talk a little bit more about the
case and the evidence the agency found
that made all the difference, and I feel
like I was meant to hear this story. That
my fight with my brother was part of a
grander scheme that put me in my car at
the exact moment when the information
I needed to help Beau would be handed
to me.

The story is winding down and I still
don't know who this magician is who
freed a wrongfully convicted man. A
truck honks at me just as the host is
thanking his guest and I catch only the
last part of his sentence before they cut to
the next segment.

"—Nash Security and Investigation."

"What city? Where?" I yell at the radio as the commercial starts. Something about getting lower insurance rates that I couldn't give two shits about.

Nash Security and Investigation. I'm thankful to have that much, at least, as I grab my cellphone to test my Google-fu and see if I can figure out where in the U.S. this Nash agency is. But I'm in the middle of the godforsaken California desert and there's no service.

I stuff my phone into my bag and pull back out onto the freeway, thinking about what I just learned. I never look for signs or believe in fate or angels or anything I can't touch, taste, see, smell, or hear, but I can't ignore the feeling deep in the pit of my stomach that I'm onto something big here. That finally there might be someone who can help me help Beau.

*

Want to read more?

➤One-click INNOCENT: EPISODE ONE Now➤

Looking for something a little sexier? Check out the RECOVERED INNO-CENCE series, starting with LIBERATE!

★Nominated in 2017 for the Romance Writers of America Rita® award★

Beau Hollis served five years in prison for a crime he didn't commit. Now he's out, but he's far from free.

Inspired by real cases taken on by The Innocence Project.

➤One-click LIBERATE Now➤

EXCERPT FROM LIBERATE

eau

B I walked out of the California Institute for Men in Chino, California two thousand, two hundred and seventy one days—nearly six years—after I walked in. I was finally free.

Free.

I don't have the same definition that most people have for that word. While I'm no longer serving a life sentence for a crime I didn't commit, I'm far from free. The repercussions of my incarceration blasted every area of my life, pitting or obliterating everything in sight. There isn't a single thing left unscarred. I don't have a home. I don't have friends. I don't have a job or any qualifications to get one. I don't have any money. I don't have the same family I had on the day of my conviction.

And I don't have Cassandra.

There's a big gaping hole in me where she once lived. Of all of the things that were taken from me she's the one thing I can never get back. I left her sleepy, naked, and sated in her bed six years ago, stealing out of her apartment with other things on my mind, unimportant things. I had an early day the next morning and needed to get home. I bent down, kissed her forehead, told her I loved her, and left.

I never saw her again.

She was brutally raped and murdered that night.

I haven't been able to take a full breath since. Not because of my subsequent arrest and conviction for her murder. That was nothing. Well, not *nothing*. It's definitely something. But it's not why I can't pull in enough air. There's a hole in my chest she used to fill. There's too much space and I can't imagine or even remember what it felt like to be whole. I've been walking around with this big, sucking chest wound since the night she died.

I'm raw yet scarred over. Little things scratch at me, reopening the wound so it never truly heals. A song. The scent of jasmine. A movie. A joke. Her name. I haven't been able to say her name out loud since I screamed it outside her apartment when her body was found and the place crawled with law enforcement personnel.

I see her everywhere. I get a glimpse of her at least once a day. Every time I turn my head I have to remind myself it's not her. It will never be her. I won't get to hold her hand, have her lay her head on my chest the way she used to or make love to her ever again. I can't call her and tell her about the stupid things that happened to me that day. She won't ever tilt her head up with the look in her eyes that was only for me. I haven't laughed in so long I'm not sure if I remember how.

My sister, Cora, thinks I should see someone, a grief councilor. I don't want to. My grief is all I have left of Cassandra. Cora doesn't understand that. No one does. I can't explain it. There are no words for what it feels like to carry it everywhere. I'm pretty sure it's the only thing holding me together. I walk around, going through the day-to-day of living, relying on those feelings to get me through. What would I have without them? Who would I be? I'm not the same man who left Cassandra's apartment that night. I'll never be him again. I shouldn't be him. I sure as shit shouldn't want to be him.

And yet...

Sometimes I wonder what it's like to be *normal*. What would happen if I took off this mantel of grief and laid it down? Would I stop seeing Cassandra everywhere? Would the smell of a common flower stop reminding me of her unique scent? Would I forget what she sounded like, her laugh, and how she felt under me? Would I lose her all over again this time forever?

The air outside of prison not only smells different, it *feels* different. I'm not used to anything resembling normal life. I'm still on prison schedule despite having been out a couple of months now. My only rebellion is letting my hair and beard grow. I don't know who that man in the mirror is. He's rougher, harder than he was six years ago. He has scars and crude tattoos jabbed into his skin by makeshift prison tattoo guns. He looks like he doesn't give a fuck about anyone or anything.

That couldn't be further from the truth.

Cora arranged for me to come to work with her. I think she's hoping it will give me something to aspire to. I'm lost. I don't recognize anyone or anything. I don't know who or what I want to be. There was a time when everything I wanted to do and be was lined up in my head just waiting for me to tick them off like a fucking checklist. Go to college. Check. Get a good paying job. Check. Marry Cassandra. Check. Buy a house. Check. Start a family. Check. Grow old with Cassandra. Check.

None of those boxes will ever be crossed off.

I have to create a new list. But where do I start? I'm twenty-four years old. I should be halfway through my checklist by now. Cora tells me I can do or be anything I want. She pushes community and technical college catalogs at me, trying to get me interested in something. At night I lay awake and attempt to imagine my life a year from now. All I see is me *still* lying on Cora's couch, *still* struggling to figure my shit out. I'm frustrating her and myself. Maybe this Take Your Brother to Work Day will give me some kind of direction even if it only helps me realize what I *don't* want to do.

I wait outside for Cora, sipping a cup of strong black coffee. I got the taste for it in prison. Before that I never touched the stuff. Cora bought me a coffee maker even though she doesn't drink it. She's been good to me. Too good. Better than I deserve. She's the reason I'm leaning against her car on a foggy San Diego morning, waiting for her instead of sitting in a prison cell wondering *why me*. She was the only person who believed in my innocence. The only one. Not even our parents—who should've stuck by me no matter what—considered for a moment that I could be innocent.

I don't know who that says more about—them or me. Cora says them, but I'm not so sure. My conviction destroyed my parents individually and as a couple. I haven't seen either one of them since shortly after being assigned a prison uniform. At first Cora made excuses for them when she visited, and then she stopped mentioning them altogether. We're supposed to have a family reunion this Sunday. Cora arranged it. She's the only reason I agreed to go. I'd do anything for her. She's more than proven she'd do anything for me. She's done *everything* for me.

Cora backs out the front door of her garage apartment, her arms full. I jog up the walk and relieve her of the files she's carrying. She locks the door and turns to me, a big smile on her face. It gets me every time. A combination of joy and surprise like she can't believe I'm really there. I can't believe it either. I hope I never get used to this feeling or that smile. I hope she doesn't either.

I follow her down the walk to her car and put her files in the trunk. I stand just in time to see the car keys flying at my face and catch them before they smack into my nose.

"You have to practice sometime," she says. "Drive us to work."

I haven't driven in six years. My license expired while I was in prison. My parents sold my car.

"Are you sure?"

She opens the passenger door and climbs in with a wink. I let out a frosty breath in the cool morning air. This is one more thing I have to relearn in my life *outside*. I slide into the driver's seat and adjust it for my bigger body and longer legs.

"The mirrors too," Cora reminds me.

It's like I'm taking Driver's Ed all over again with my little sister as my teacher. I hope driving isn't as hard as riding a bike. That shit took me too many tries to get right. I'm wobbly like a kid riding without training wheels for the first time. Bike riding is a fucked up metaphor for my life now. Everything is an uphill struggle and scary as fuck. I suck so bad at it I wonder sometimes if I shouldn't just commit a crime for real this time so I can go back to the predictability and reliability of prison life. I won't, but the thought is scarily tempting sometimes.

You wouldn't think being free would be so hard.

I do as Cora instructs and start the car. She coaches me the whole way. I'm relieved when we arrive safely. Driving is a hell of a lot easier than riding a bike. We get out of the car and head into the offices of Nash Security and Investigation. I owe Cora and everyone in this place *everything.* If Mr. Nash and his son, Leo, hadn't agreed to help Cora find the bastard who killed Cassandra and worked to set me free, I'd still be sitting in a cell. How do you repay someone who rescued you from hell and gave you your life back?

I juggle Cora's files that I retrieved from the trunk, open the door for her, and follow her inside. The receptionist, Savannah, looks up at Cora, then does a double take when she spies me trailing behind my sister. Her first, fleeting glance is full of female appreciation that quickly morphs into avid curiosity tinged with fear. She doesn't want to be attracted to an ex-con, but I'd put money on her panties being soaked at the thought of fucking me. I'm a walking, talking good girl's bad boy dream. I'm the guy she bangs once or twice on the quiet just so she can brag about it later to her friends.

I grin at Savannah, following it with a wink and lick of the lips. She gasps and presses her hands to her chest, her cheeks bloom red. If we were alone I bet I could take her right there on top of her desk. Wouldn't even have to pull her panties all the way down, just push up her skirt and pull them aside. She'd shower after, feeling dirty, later she'd jack off reliving it. I'm not even slightest bit tempted by her or any other woman I've met since I got out. Another way my life's fucked up.

I set Cora's files down where she directs me. Her office is small with two desks in the middle facing each other. It's an odd arrangement, but Cora likes it this way I guess.

She gestures to the desk opposite hers. "Have a seat." She sifts through her pile of files until she finds what she's looking for, then pulls it out and comes around to where I'm sitting. "I thought maybe I'd start you off with some simple searches." She twitches the mouse, bringing the computer screen to life. "These are the search sites we use."

Clicking on the top three bookmarked sites, she brings them up, explaining how they use them and what info they can provide. She has me do some easy searches, then leaves me on my own. I don't suck at it. I'm actually quite good. And I like the work. I'm half way through the searches Cora wanted me to do when Savannah sticks her head in the door.

"Your ten o'clock is here," she tells Cora, her gaze darts to me then back to Cora.

"Thanks, Savannah. Want to sit in?" Cora asks me. "Take a break from the computer?"

"Sure." I stand and stretch.

Savannah jumps and squeaks, then disappears from the doorway.

Cora's mouth bends into a frown. "I don't know what's wrong with her lately."

"Don't you?"

"I'll talk to her."

"Leave it."

I follow Cora into the reception area. Savannah blocks whoever it is she's talking to so I can't see who it is, but whoever they are they're small, much smaller than Savannah's five-nine frame. Savannah shifts, revealing a pastel confection of a young woman about Cora's age.

All lace and silk, she's sweet looking in her soft colors like she just walked out of a Sunday church service. But the look in her eyes is wary...guarded...jaded, reminding me of angry, hard prison stares. This chick's seen some shit. More than that, she's experienced some shit, has maybe even done some shit. She's a survivor. This I understand. I recognize her in the same way I recognize the new man that stares back at me in the mirror.

Her costume is nearly perfect. I bet if I sniffed her she'd smell like baby powder and lemons. I edge closer to her. She catches me with a sudden flick of a glance, freezing me where I stand. Everything about her shouts *back the fuck off*. It only makes me want to draw closer. Who is she? Who or what made her this way? And why does she look at me like she knows who I am? Not the TV news segment me, but the real me, the Beau deep, down inside.

For the first time since I got out of

prison I don't feel alone. There really are others out there like me. One of them is standing mere feet in front of me, regarding me with the same guarded, expectant look I'm wearing.

And she's *beautiful*.

★Nominated in 2017 for the Romance Writers of America Rita® award★

➤One-click LIBERATE Now➤

LOOKING for something lighter and funnier? Check out THE MISADVEN-TURES OF MAGGIE MAE series, starting with WAKE UP, MAGGIE, available now! Maggie has to keep her very inappropriate thoughts to herself about the FBI Special Agent assigned to protect her from a murderer.

➤One-click   WAKE   UP, MAGGIE Now➤

ACKNOWLEDGMENTS

Authors need people around them who speak the same crazy and the ladies of LIR are my tribe. It was a tough year of mostly not writing, but you kept dragging me along and I appreciate every single one of you for it. I couldn't have survived without your support.

My boys (who are really MEN—or at least man-sized) have suffered through the teasing about their mom's sex books and have supported my writing every step of the way. Love you, boys!

Episode Two

Episode Three

The Misadventures of Maggie Mae

Wake Up, Maggie

You're Mine, Maggie

Find Me, Maggie

Azalea March Mysteries

Dyed and Gone

Beth Writing as Betty Paper

Exposed

Captive

Tinsel

Piano Lessons

BETH'S BOOKS FOR WRITERS

Crafting Unputdownable Fiction series

Going Deep Into Deep Point of View

Making Description Work Hard For You

Some Like It Hot: Writing Sex and Romance

ABOUT THE AUTHOR

USA Today best selling author and Rita®
finalist, Beth Yarnall, writes mysteries,
romantic suspense, and the occasional
hilarious tweet. She lives in Southern
California with her husband, two sons,
and their rescue dogs where she is hard at
work on her next novel. For more information about Beth and her novels please
visit her website- www.bethyarnall.com

f facebook.com/bethyarnallauthor

a amazon.com/author/bethyarnall

BB bookbub.com/authors/beth-yarnall

www.ingramcontent.com/pod-product-compliance
Lightning Source LLC
Chambersburg PA
CBHW030459130626
46549CB00007B/2791